Mai ...ays monsters

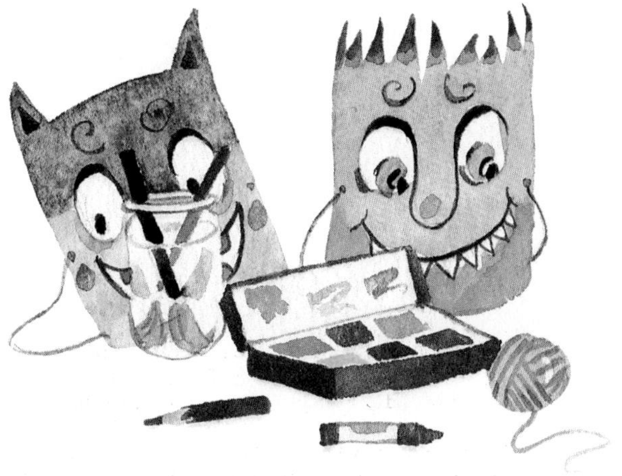

by Wendy Body and Stan Cullimore

Illustrated by Rhian Nest James

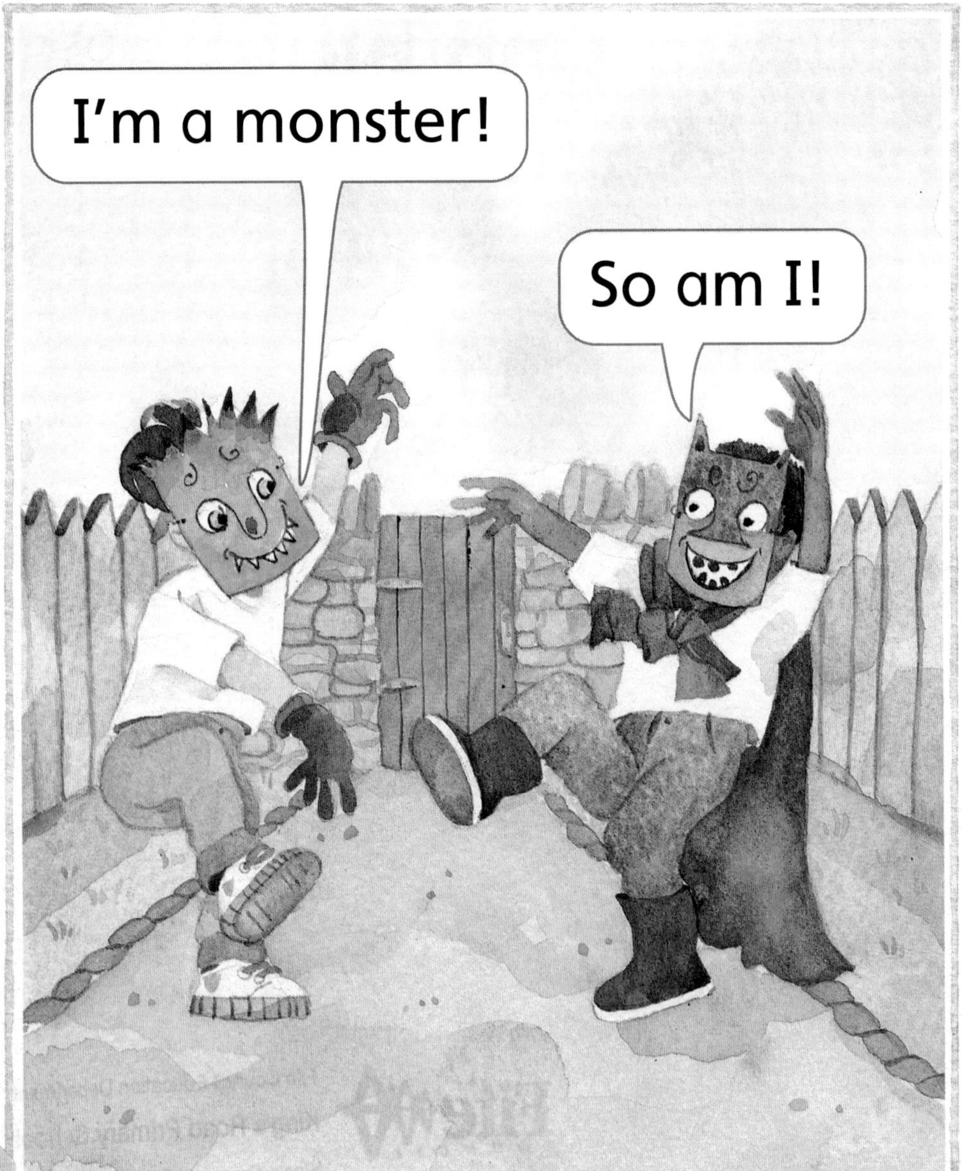
I'm a monster!
So am I!

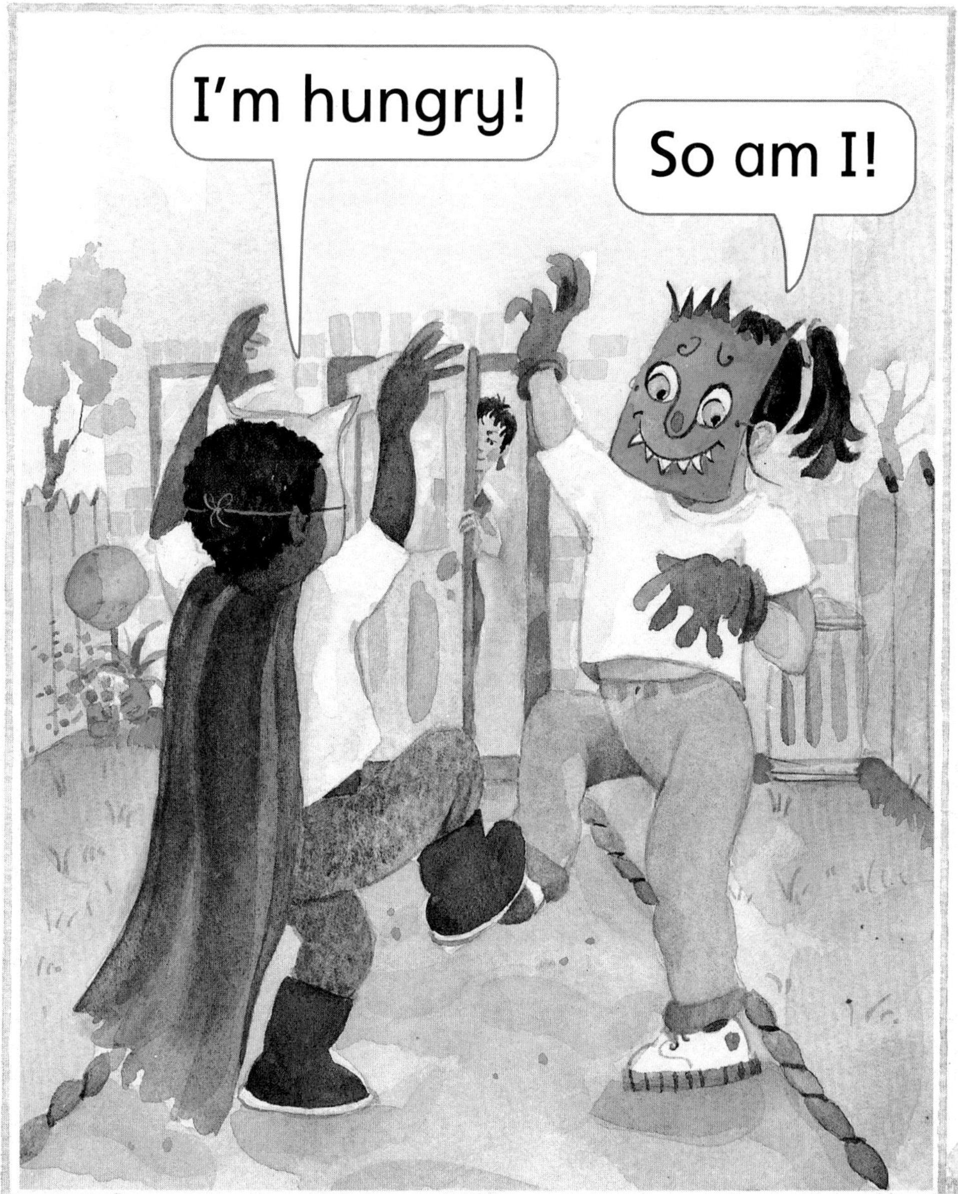
I'm hungry!
So am I!

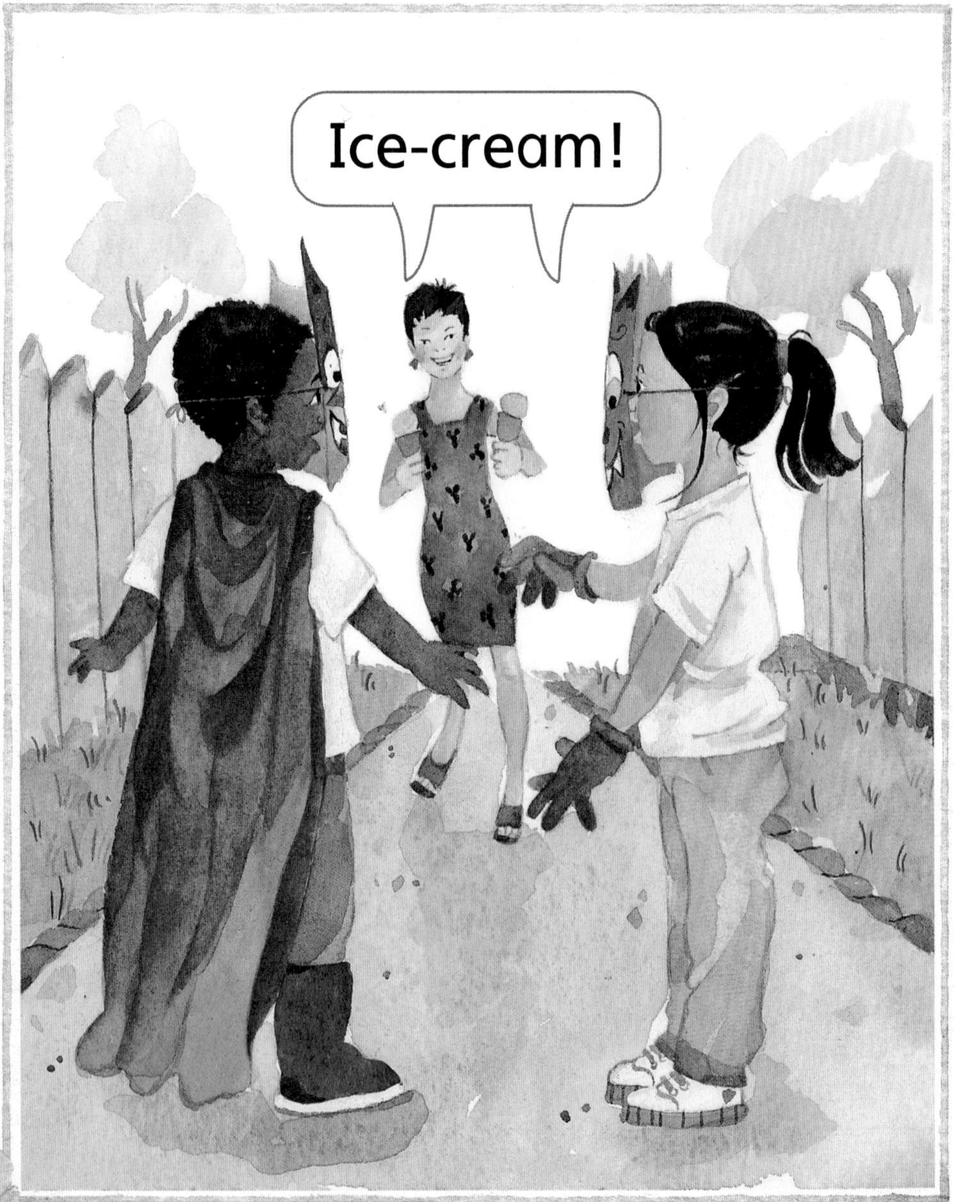
Ice-cream!

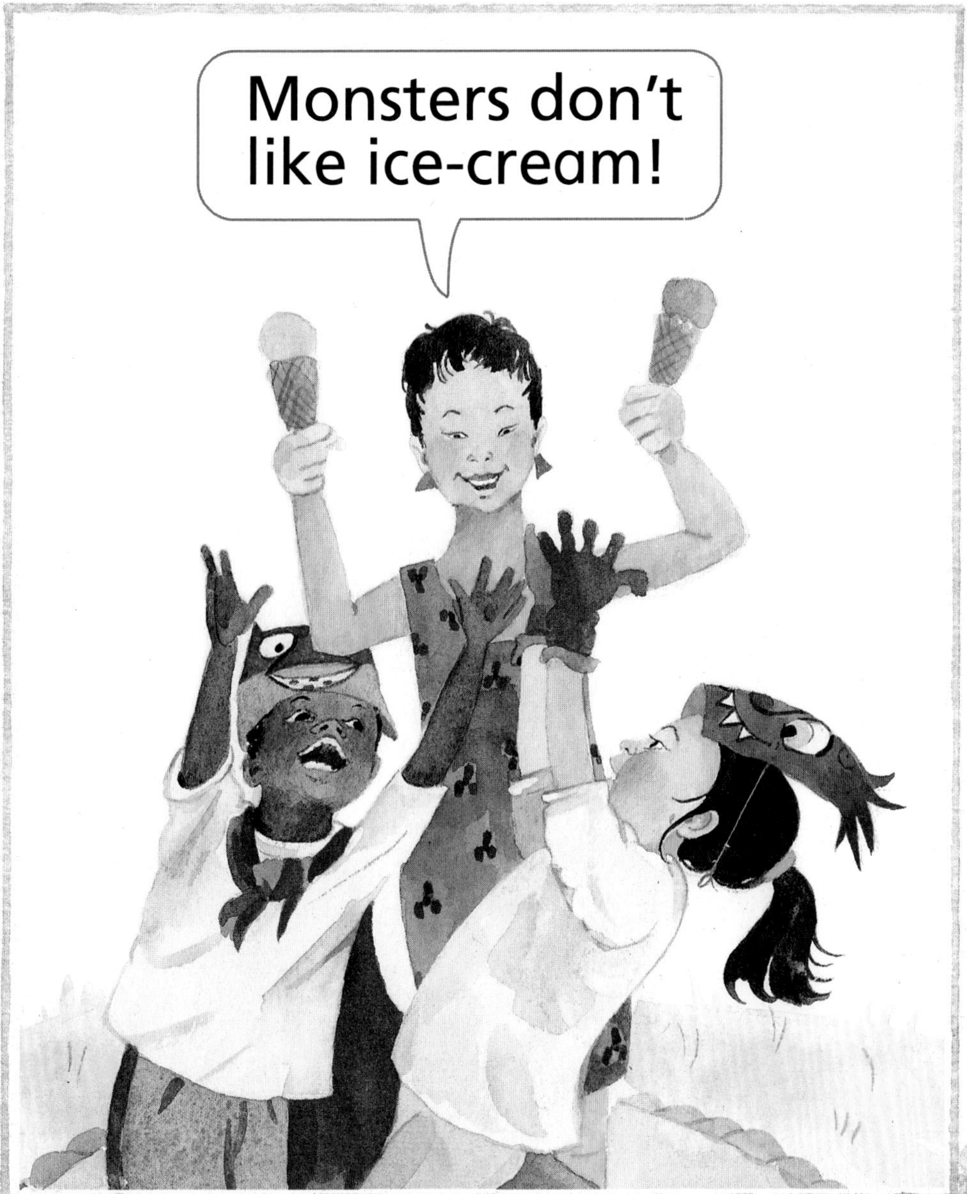
Monsters don't like ice-cream!

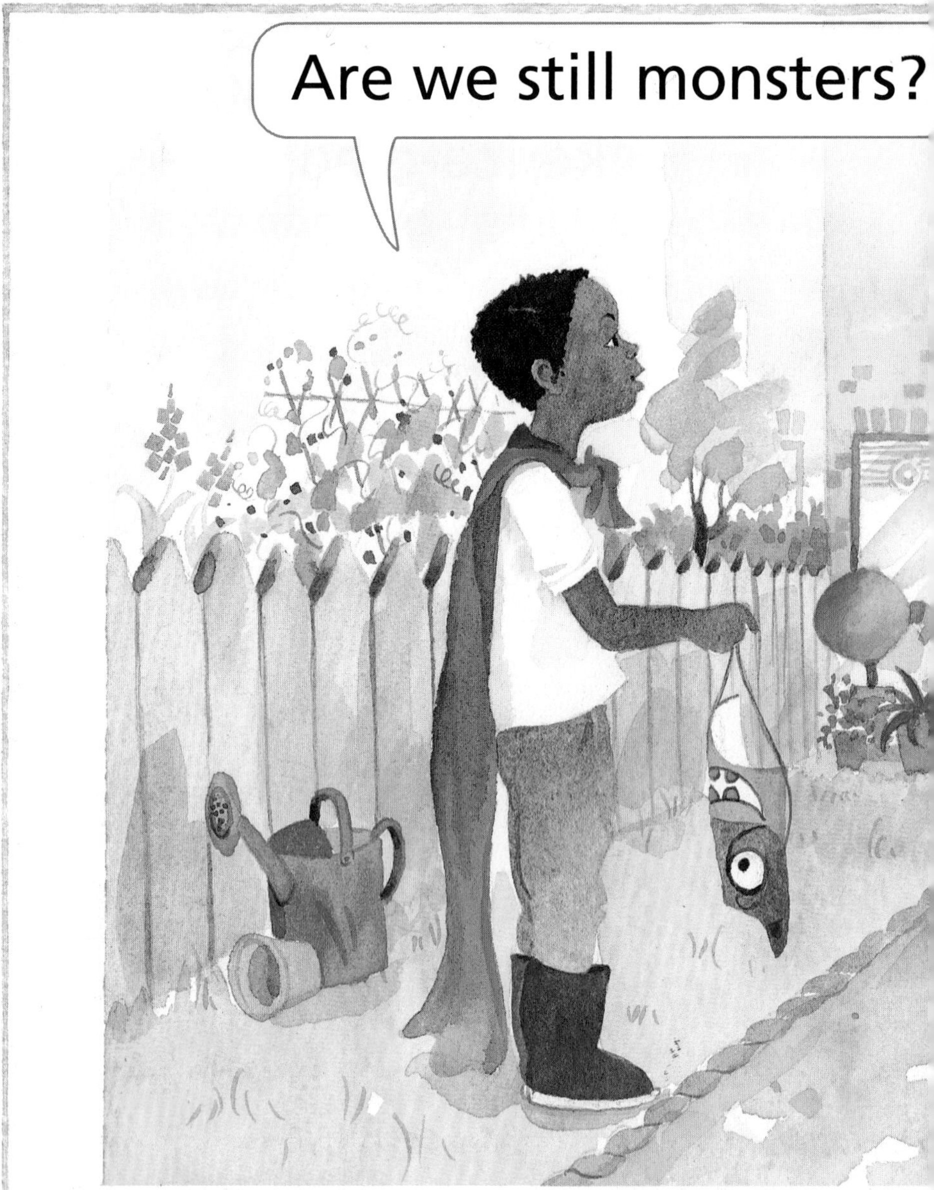
Are we still monsters?

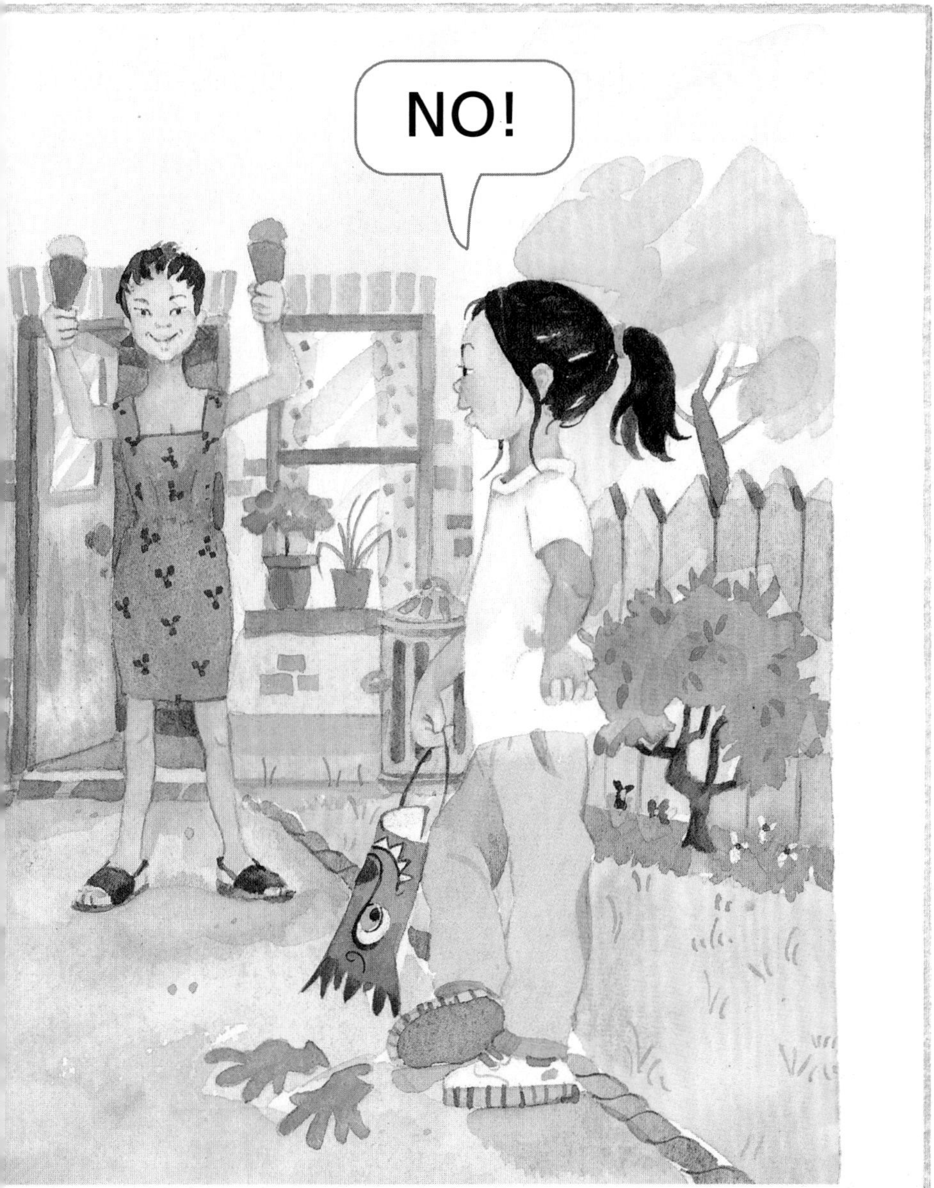
NO!

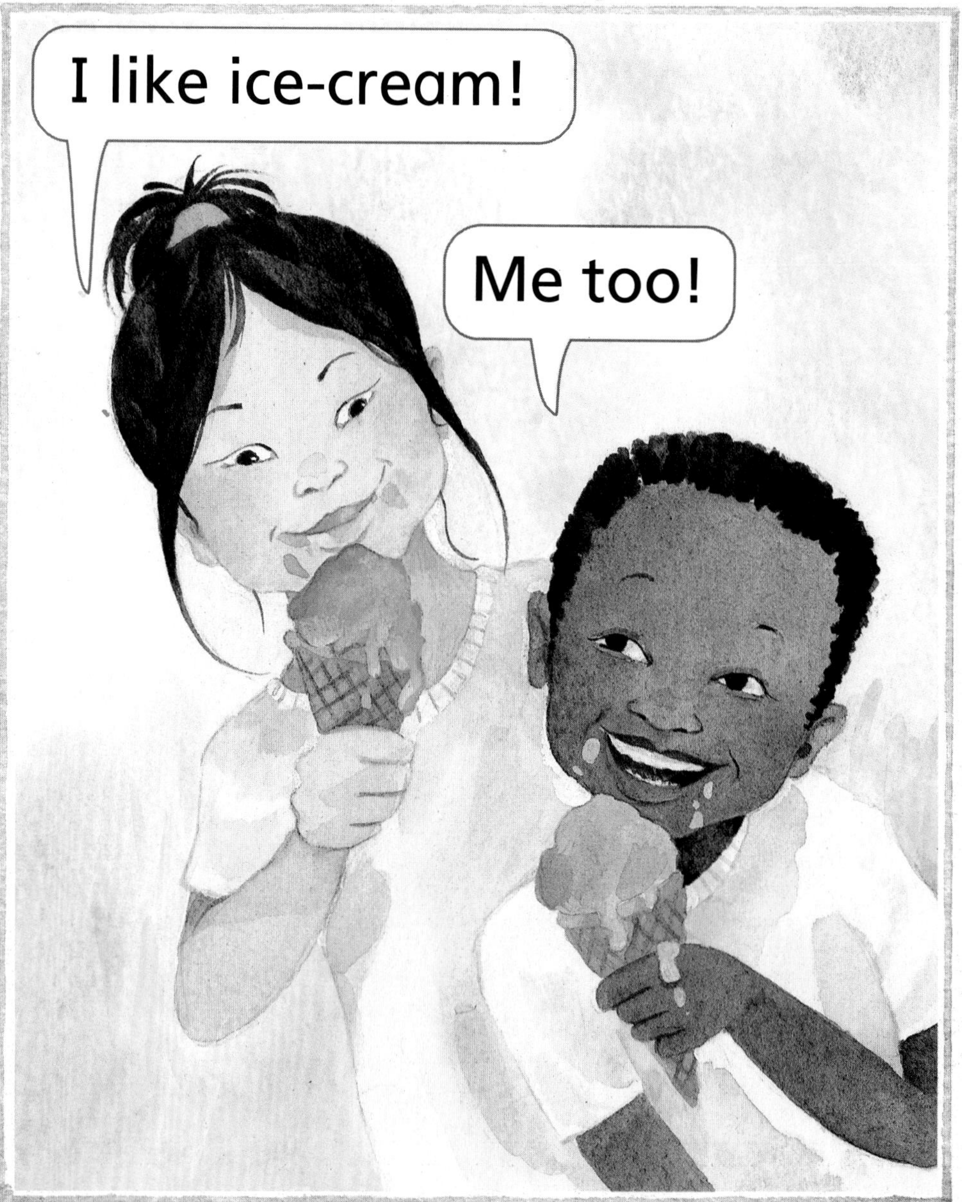
I like ice-cream!
Me too!